Robinson Cano shows off his picture-perfect swing at the plate.

Chien Ming-Wang stares down the batter before throwing his sinker for a groundball out.

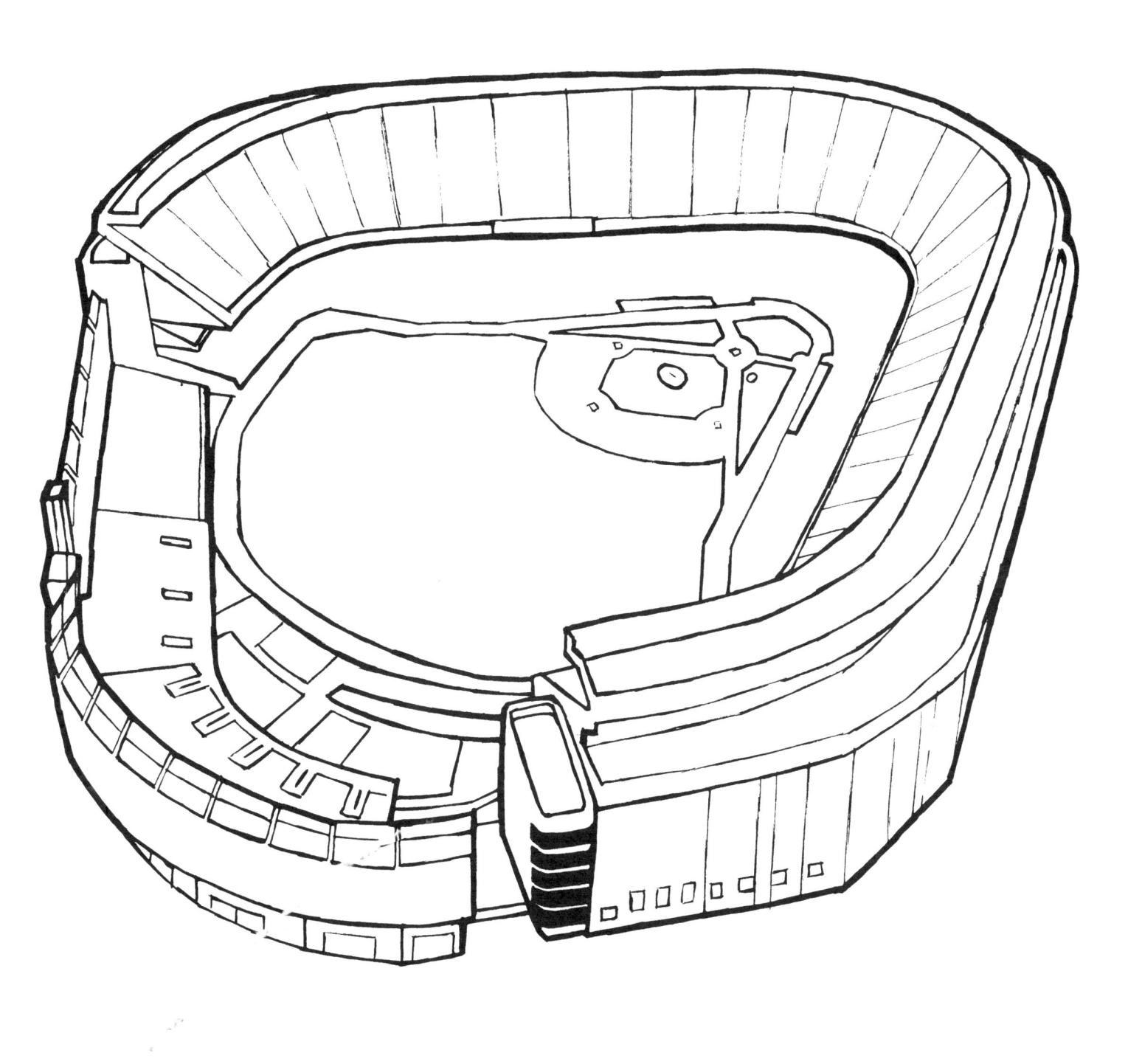

Yankee Stadium®, hallowed as "The House That Ruth Built™", is a national treasure.

Use your knowledge about *Yankee Stadium* to solve the following crossword puzzle.

Crossword Puzzle 1 - *Yankee Stadium* Facts

Across

1. What team did the Yankees buy the Babe from?

3. Joe DiMaggio had a 56 game _____ streak in 1941.

4. In the original Yankee Stadium dimensions, the left-center wall was 460 ft. from home. This area of the park was nicknamed after a famous California desert. (2 words)

5. This event, which decides the World Series championship, has taken place at Yankee Stadium more than any other park. (2 words)

7. Don Larsen is the only pitcher to throw one of these in a World Series championship, retiring all 27 batters he faced. (2 words)

11. The Yankees have their own Hall of Fame to honor their greatest players, managers, and executives. It is located behind the left-center fence and is called _____ Park.

13. What borough of New York City do the Yankees call home?

14. Before they were called the Yankees, they were the _____.

15. These were added to Yankee Stadium in 1946, so the Yankees could play at night.

Down

2. Before moving to New York, the franchise played in Baltimore and were the original Baltimore _____.

4. Though officially meaning "a succession of rulers", this word is used to describe the Yankees continuing dominance.

6. This player's skyrocketing popularity ensured large crowds, so Yankee Stadium is often called, "The House That _____ Built."

7. Before building Yankee Stadium, The Yankees shared the _____ Grounds with the New York Giants. They were asked to leave when more fans started to come to Yankees games than Giants games!

8. The record-setting Yankees offense of 1927 was known by the violent nickname of _____ Row.

9. When the Yankees played the Mets in 2000, it was called the ____ Series, after a popular mode of NYC transportation.

10. This NFL team called Yankee Stadium home from 1956-1973. They now play in East Rutherford, NJ.

12. Wally _____ was the last Yankees player to start at first base before Gehrig began his record setting consecutive games streak.

Use your knowledge about *Yankee Stadium* to solve the following crossword puzzle.

Crossword Puzzle 1 - *Yankee Stadium* Facts

Solution is on page 53.

- 5 -

Connect-the-Dots #1

Connnect the dots to reveal what's on these pinstripes!

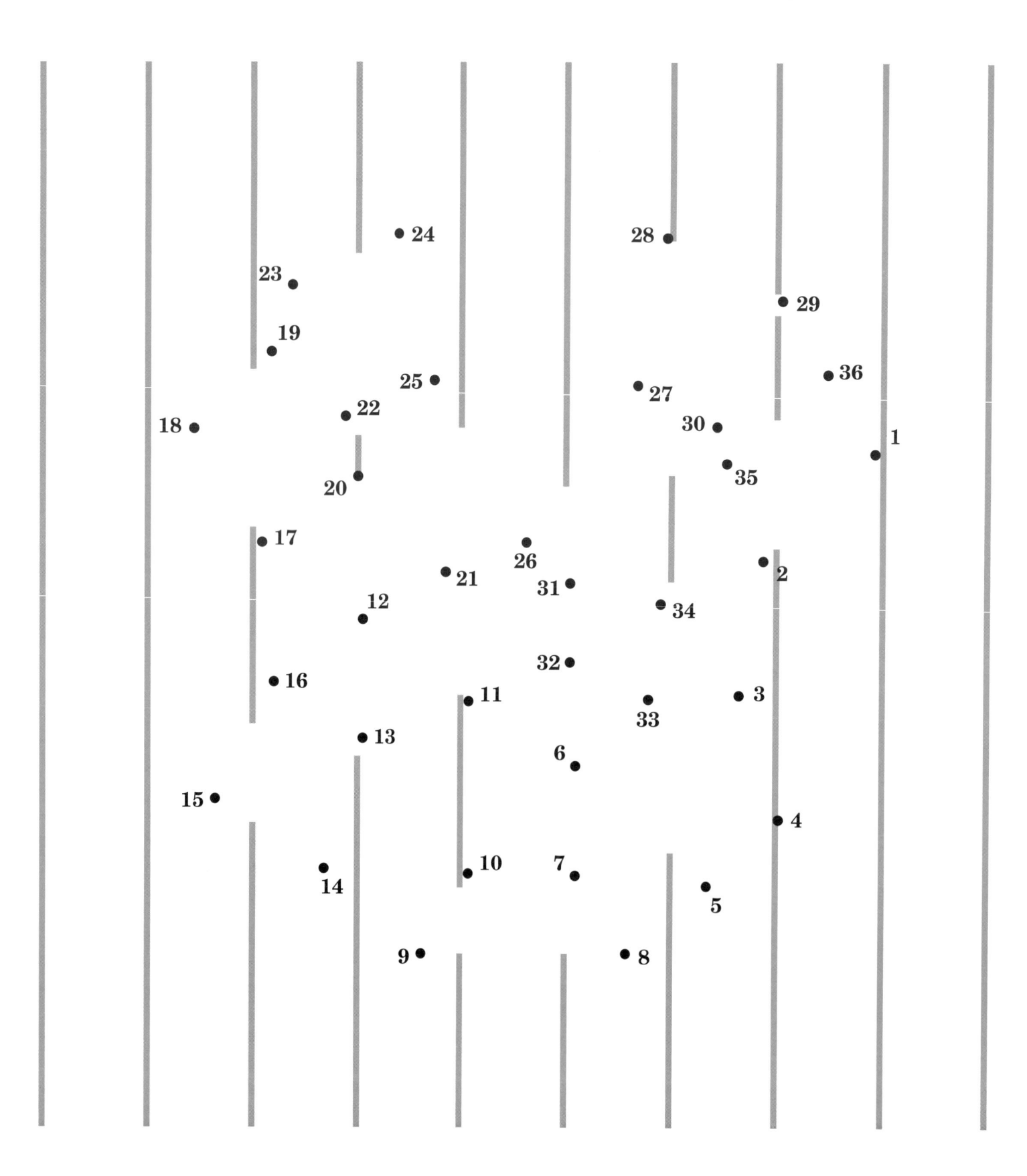

Captain Derek Jeter does his best work in the late innings and most important games.

Melky Cabrera scales the wall to snatch away a sure home run from the opposition.

Word Search #1
The Greatest *Yankees* Players

```
B Z W M H O V A U F Y V N E N L E U H G
N Q G H J R F Q R C G L T T Y W O T O F
W M U E U B K W R E L S G P C Q Q M Q F
I R Z N H N H D R I O G J N U Z E C V O
N X O V L R T W H V Z D X H I Z A G P R
F R U T H B I E E N T Z Y Q A T Y U E D
I M O O Y B C G R D J P U B T H T S T A
E E P R I J A C K S O N E T V D O A K L
L T T M Q G J M Q H T I E N O Y S K M L
D T N B A S G Y E K C I D M X I H Z G I
S I Q O C R J A Z V B Q A S R O O V Q E
W T V T S V T M M E V N W A W O G P E N
V T E B K N N I R I T F M A V B E R J O
W E R U Q L U R N L D G R L P B C C H Y
P P G A O M A M E R U D H P N X I N A D
U W X T E J Z B G U I D R Y V T T B D G
```

Try to find all the words contained in the list below: (Hint: Words may be found by looking up and down, across, or diagonally. Some words are even spelled backwards!)

RUTH	MANTLE	FORD	HOWARD	PETTITTE
DIMAGGIO	BERRA	MATTINGLY	DICKEY	WINFIELD
GEHRIG	RIZZUTO	JACKSON	ONEILL	GOMEZ
MARIS	MUNSON	MARTIN	GUIDRY	HUNTER

Solution is on page 53.

- 9 -

2008 *Yankees* Player Challenge
Yankees Roster effective April 1, 2008

No	PITCHERS	B	T	HT	WT	DOB
63	Jonathan Albaladejo	R	R	6-5	260	10/30/82
33	Brian Bruney	R	R	6-3	235	02/17/82
62	Joba Chamberlain	R	R	6-2	230	09/23/85
48	Kyle Farnsworth	R	R	6-4	235	04/14/76
21	LaTroy Hawkins	R	R	6-5	215	12/21/72
34	Phil Hughes	R	R	6-5	230	06/24/86
31	Ian Kennedy	R	R	6-0	195	12/19/84
35	Mike Mussina	L	R	6-2	190	12/08/68
39	Ross Ohlendorf	R	R	6-4	235	08/08/82
42	Mariano Rivera	R	R	6-2	185	11/29/69
61	Billy Traber	L	L	6-5	205	09/18/79
40	Chien-Ming Wang	R	R	6-3	225	03/31/80

No	CATCHERS	B	T	HT	WT	DOB
26	Jose Molina	R	R	6-2	235	06/03/75
20	Jorge Posada	S	R	6-2	215	08/17/71

No	INFIELDERS	B	T	HT	WT	DOB
14	Wilson Betemit	S	R	6-3	230	11/02/81
24	Robinson Cano	L	R	6-0	205	10/22/82
17	Shelley Duncan	R	R	6-5	225	09/29/79
11	Morgan Ensberg	R	R	6-2	210	08/26/75
2	Derek Jeter	R	R	6-3	195	06/26/74
13	Alex Rodriguez	R	R	6-3	225	07/27/75

No	OUTFIELDERS	B	T	HT	WT	DOB
53	Bobby Abreu	L	R	6-0	210	03/11/74
28	Melky Cabrera	S	L	5-11	200	08/11/84
18	Johnny Damon	L	L	6-2	205	11/05/73
55	Hideki Matsui	L	R	6-2	210	06/12/74

No	DESIGNATED HITTERS	B	T	HT	WT	DOB
25	Jason Giambi	L	R	6-3	235	01/08/71

2008 *Yankees* Player Challenge

Use the names on the *Yankees* roster to fill in the correct players who accomplished these milestones.

1. _____ blasted home his 500th career home run in August of 2007.

2. _____ is a switch hitter that has made it to the MLB® All-Star Game® five times without using batting gloves!

3. Yankees captain _____ snagged his third Gold Glove award in 2006.

4. _____ didn't join the team until late July in 2006 but still found time to rack up 42 RBI for the Yankees.

5. _____ was voted to start the 2006 MLB All-Star Game at second base by the fans, but couldn't play due to injury.

6. _____ is a two-time All-Star who came over from the rival team to roam centerfield for the Yankees in 2006.

7. By playing in every one of his first 518 games in the Major Leagues™, _____ earned the MLB® record for most consecutive games played to start a career.

8. _____ earned the "This Week In Baseball" Most Outstanding Catch of the Year Award in 2006 for his famous home run robbing grab. It cost Manny Ramirez a HR and caused teammate Johnny Damon to dance in celebration.

9. _____ may be most concerned about throwing strikes, but he's a sure-handed fielder as well, as shown by his astounding six Gold Gloves.

10. Hailing from Taiwan, _____ established himself as a Yankees ace in 2006, winning 19 games with a 3.63 ERA.

11. Lefty _____ picked up four World Series rings with the Yankees. Bronx Bombers™ fans everywhere rejoiced when he returned for the 2007 season.

12. _____ is the Yankees most feared reliever. His devastating cutter has caused many broken bats during his brilliant career.

Solution is on page 54.

Use your knowledge about current *Yankees* players to solve the following crossword puzzle.

Crossword Puzzle 2 - *Yankees* Players

Across

3 This rightfielder hit .330 after joining the Yankees before the trading deadline in 2006.

5 Once this player was done dominating Japanese baseball he came to the Yankees to play left field.

9 This Yankees all-star catcher has been with the team his entire career.

11 This dependable starter pitched for the Orioles before coming to the Yankees in 2001.

12 This second basemen earned an All Star selection in only his second year in the Majors™.

14 This lefty hurler was a fan favorite during the Yankees World Series victories. He rejoined the team in 2007.

16 This infielder was a starter for the Yankees 2004 playoff run. He rejoined the team in 2006 and has become a trusted utility player.

17 This Taiwanese pitcher won 19 games in 2006.

18 This 2005 AL MVP shifted from shortstop to third base for the Yankees upon being traded in 2004.

Down

1 This reliever led the Majors in appearances in 2006. He entered 83 games.

2 This rookie hurler was cruising towards a no-hitter against the Rangers in his second Major League start before leaving with an injury.

4 This Yankees closer is considered by many to be the best of all-time.

6 This 6' 4" set-up man appeared in 72 games and recorded 75 Ks in 2006, his first year with the Yankees.

7 In 2006, his first full season, this outfielder hit a solid .280 and played all three outfield positions.

8 This former "caveman" came over from the Yankees' rivals to hit lead-off and handle center field.

10 This imposing first basemen and DH had 350 homers coming into the 2007 season.

12 This "Rocket" returned in May 2007 to the team where he won a World Series in 2000.

13 This star shortstop's clutch play in a delayed World Series game earned him the nickname "Mr. November."

15 This Yankees manager led the team to four World Series championships.

Use your knowledge about current *Yankees* players to solve the following crossword puzzle.

Crossword Puzzle 2 - *Yankees* Players

Solution is on page 54.

"The Moose" Mike Mussina uses his pin-point control to zero in on his catcher's spot.

Focused Alex Rodriguez follows the flight of a home run out of Yankee Stadium.

Gold Glove winning shortstop Derek Jeter makes another tough throw to first.

You Make the Call #1

Ball or strike? Fair or Foul? Safe or Out? Usually, the umpires have to make the tough decisions, but now... YOU MAKE THE CALL!

Here's the situation...

Mariano Rivera is in trouble. The normally dominant closer has run into some difficulty against the potent Pirates lineup during an Interleague Play contest. After recording the first two outs quickly, Pirates player Jason Bay smacked a double. Now Adam LaRoche steps up representing the tying run. LaRoche works the count full. On a 3-2 pitch, Posada gives his closer a sign—no surprise, Jorge wants the cutter. Against lefties like LaRoche, Rivera's cutter tends to break in at the last second, making many swings end in broken bats and easy outs. However, this time the cutter is almost too good; its break is so sharp that, although LaRoche swings at it, it cuts in so drastically that it hits him on the hand. LaRoche smiles, and trots down to first, thinking he just earned a base against one of the toughest pitchers in baseball history. But wait—the umpire calls him back. What's the umpire going to say?

Solution is on page 54.

Solve the *Yankees* Scramble

Unscramble the letters below to reveal *Yankees* words or phrases:

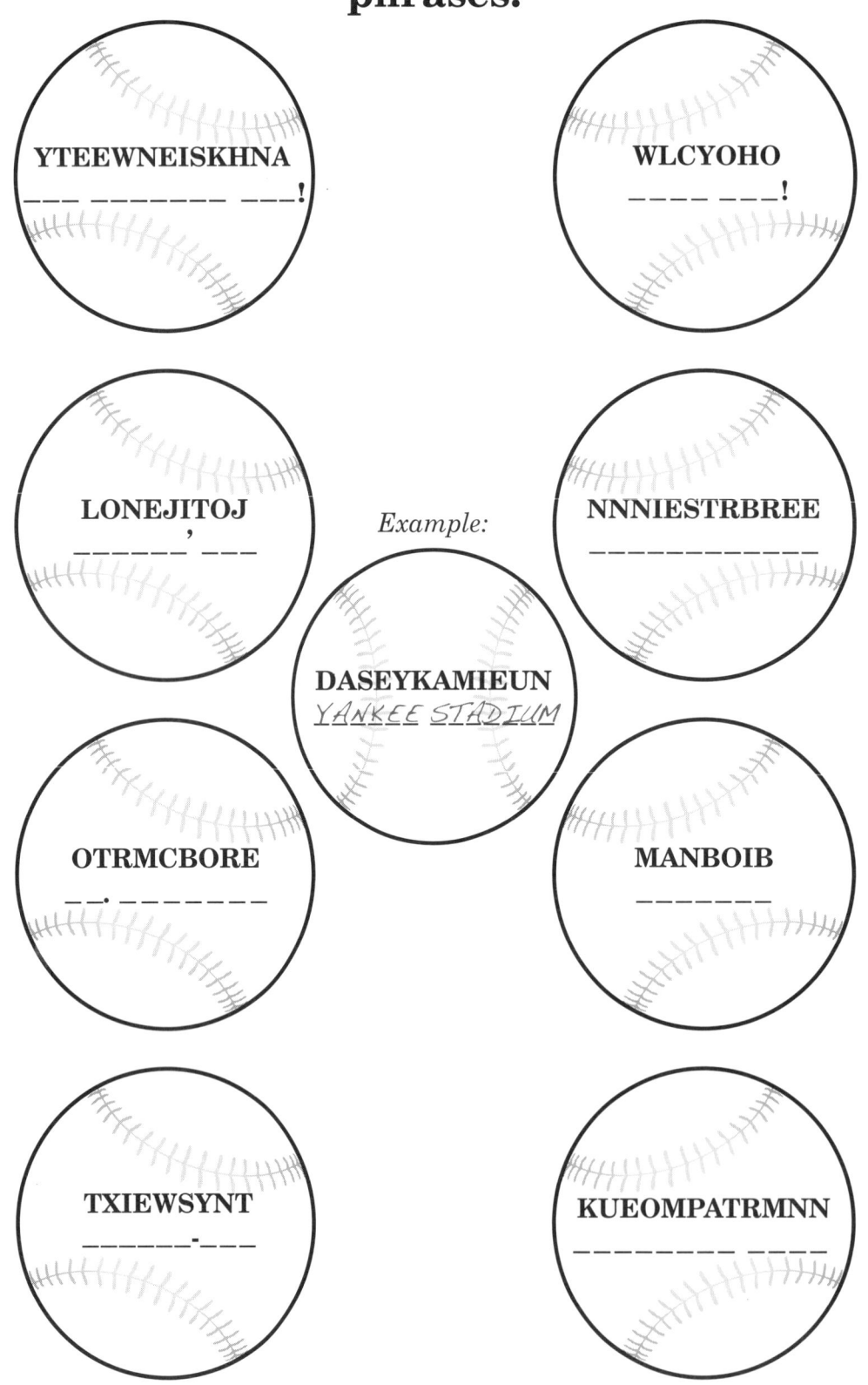

YTEEWNEISKHNA
___ _____ ___!

WLCYOHO
____ ___!

LONEJITOJ
_____'___

NNNIESTRBREE
_____

Example:

DASEYKAMIEUN
YANKEE STADIUM

OTRMCBORE
__._____

MANBOIB
_____

TXIEWSYNT
_____-___

KUEOMPATRMNN
_____ ____

Solution is on page 55.

Jorge Posada uses his whole body to make a clutch catch behind the plate.

Yankees Nicknames Challenge

Match these famous Yankees nicknames to the players (from the past and present) that appear on the next page:

- "Scooter"
- "Sandman"
- "The Mick"
- "El Duque"
- "Iron Horse"
- "Donnie Baseball"
- "Goose"
- "Sultan of Swat" / "The Bambino"
- "Eye Chart"
- "Moose"
- "Louisiana Lightning"
- "Leche"
- "Boomer"
- "A-Rod"
- "Caveman"
- "Rocket"
- "Mr. October"
- "Chairman of the Board"
- "Giambino"
- "Yankee Clipper"
- "Catfish"

Yankees Nicknames Challenge

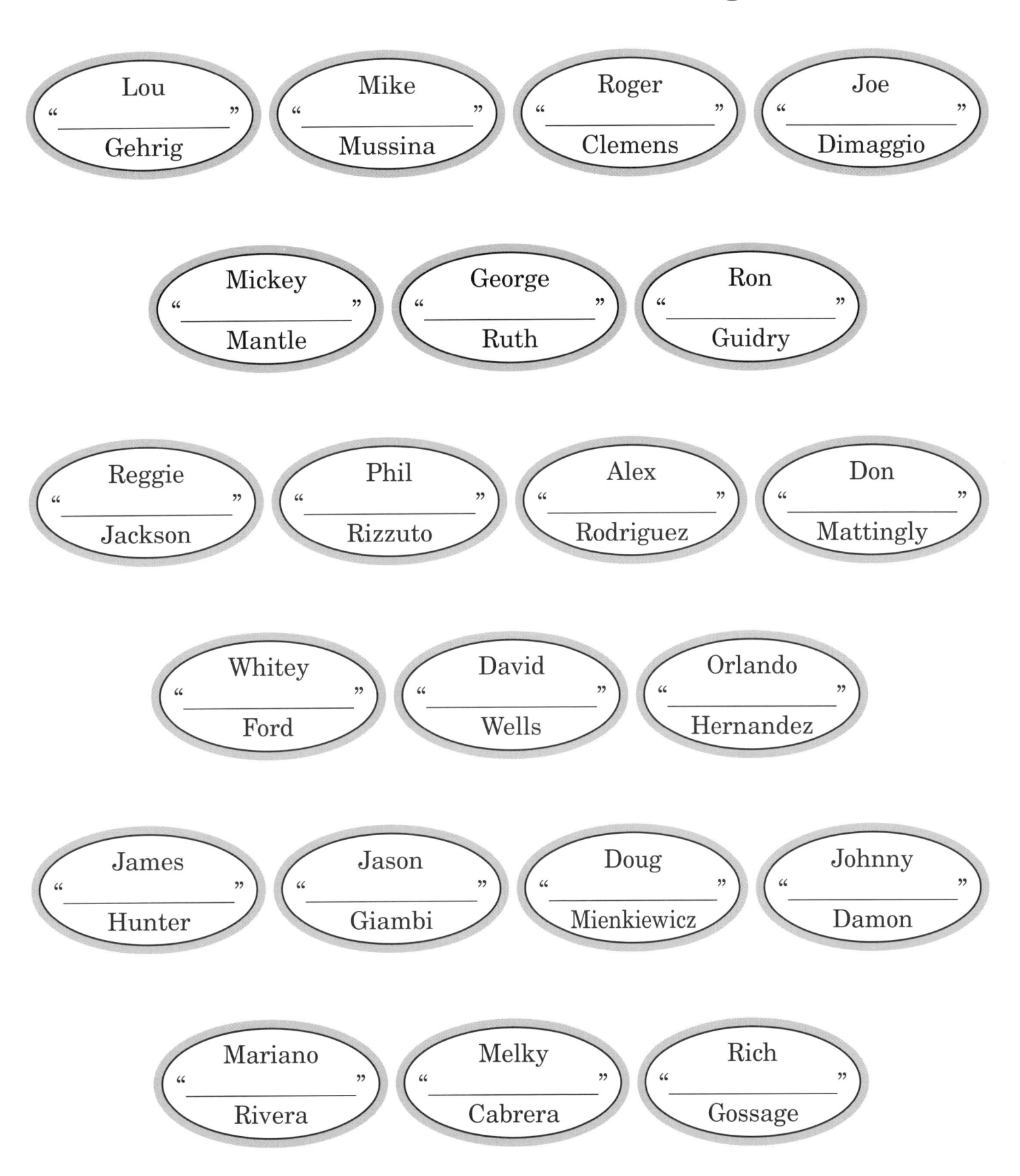

| Lou "_____" Gehrig | Mike "_____" Mussina | Roger "_____" Clemens | Joe "_____" Dimaggio |

| Mickey "_____" Mantle | George "_____" Ruth | Ron "_____" Guidry |

| Reggie "_____" Jackson | Phil "_____" Rizzuto | Alex "_____" Rodriguez | Don "_____" Mattingly |

| Whitey "_____" Ford | David "_____" Wells | Orlando "_____" Hernandez |

| James "_____" Hunter | Jason "_____" Giambi | Doug "_____" Mienkiewicz | Johnny "_____" Damon |

| Mariano "_____" Rivera | Melky "_____" Cabrera | Rich "_____" Gossage |

Solution is on page 55.

- 21 -

Use your knowledge about *Yankees* history to solve the following crossword puzzle.

Crossword Puzzle 3 - *Yankees* Dynasty

Across

2 This lefty pitcher played for all 4 championship teams and is tied for the most playoff wins with 13.

5 This player was the Mets ace in the late 80's. He came to the Yankees in 1996 and pitched a no-hitter. He stayed until 1997 and also returned for part of the 2000 season.

8 This pitcher won the 1994 American League Cy Young Award for the Royals, as well 4 championship rings with the Yanks. His fans called themselves "Coneheads."

9 This player was nicknamed "The King". He is best known for his 3-run homer off Mark Wohlers in game 4 of the 1996 World Series.

12 This portly pitcher came to the Yankees in 1997, and pitched a perfect game against the Twins in 1998. He left in 1999, but returned to the team for the 2002 and 2003 seasons.

13 This large first baseman/DH was a star for the Detroit Tigers, where he hit 51 home runs in 1990. He played for the 1996 World Series team.

14 This second baseman starred for the Twins before joining the Yankees in 1998. He won three rings, but had some infamous fielding difficulties starting in 1999.

15 This reliable relief pitcher played for the Yankees from 1997-2002 as a left handed specialist.

16 This starting third baseman played for the Yankees from 1998-2000. Before that, he played for the A's.

Down

1 This outfielder/DH was a star for the New York Mets teams of the late 80's. He played for the Yankees from 1995-1999.

3 This is the nickname of the Cuban pitcher who came to the Yankees in 1998. He would become an extremely reliable post season pitcher on his way to winning three rings. (2 words)

4 This fiery right fielder came to the Yankees from the Reds in 1993, and remained a fixture in the lineup until 2001. He hit .359 to win the batting title in 1994.

6 This "Rocket" was a star for the Red Sox and Blue Jays before joining the Yankees in 1999. He left in 2003, but returned to the Yankees starting lineup in 2007.

7 This player, usually a DH for the Yankees, starred for the Braves then Indians before joining the Yankees during the 2000 season. He would leave after 2001.

10 This pitcher won 4 rings with the Yankees as a sometime starter and dependable reliever. He also won a ring with the Red Sox in 2004, and is the only active player to have won a ring with both the Yankees and Red Sox.

11 This player was a catcher for the Yankees from 1996-1999. He is now a Yankees broadcaster.

Use your knowledge about *Yankees* history to solve the following crossword puzzle.

Crossword Puzzle 3 - *Yankees* Dynasty

Solution is on page 56.

- 23 -

As one of the premier leadoff hitters in baseball, Johnny Damon uses both his power and speed to record another extra-base hit.

Mariano Rivera prepares to unleash a bat-breaking late inning pitch.

International Game

Dominican Republic   Puerto Rico   Venezuela

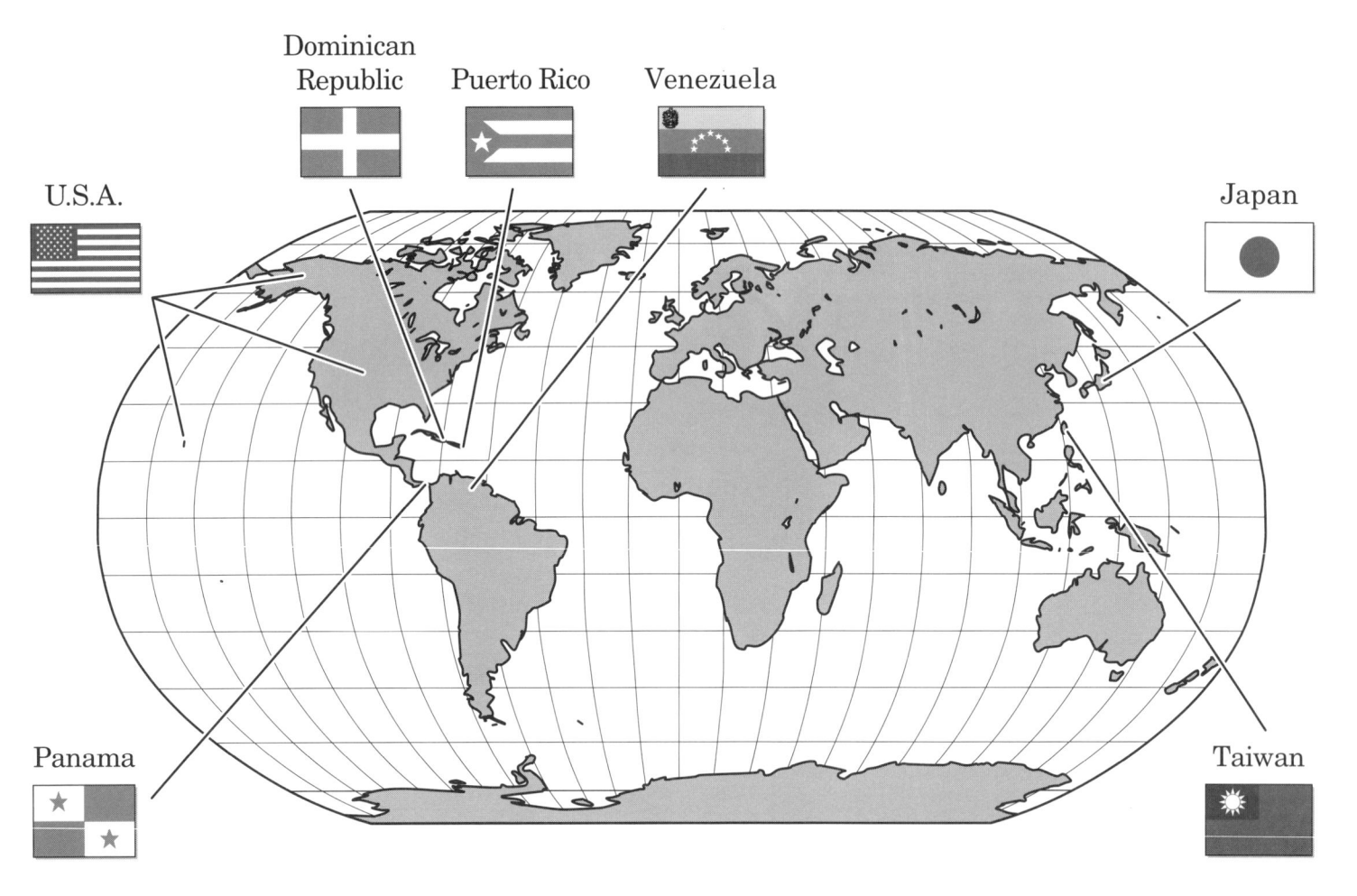

U.S.A.   Japan

Panama   Taiwan

Baseball is an international game. Match these Yankees players with their countries of origin. Write each player's name on the next page, below the flag of the country where he was born.

Johnny Damon
Jorge Posada
Jason Giambi
Chien-Ming Wang
Joba Chamberlain
Melky Cabrera

Bobby Abreu
Mariano Rivera
Robinson Cano
Alex Rodriguez
Hideki Matsui
Derek Jeter

International Game

Write each player's name from the previous page below the flag of the country where he was born:

U.S.A.

Example: Derek Jeter
_____
_____
_____
_____

Panama

_____

Puerto Rico

_____

Venezuela

_____

Japan

_____

Dominican Republic

_____
_____

Taiwan

_____

Solution is on page 56.

After he strikes out the side, Joba Chamberlain celebrates just as hard as he throws.

New Yankees skipper Joe Girardi oversees the action from the bench.

Word Search #2
October Baseball

```
S K J D W S M V I L L A I N S V E X V T
S K P I E T N A C I R E M A G J P I L V
X H M S P H L P Y O T N M F E C G S U A
C R R N O I S I V I D A M S R R B Y L L
I U E S F S K J C V B T D W M E V T E L
C Z Z M G P E Y S T L I F S S F H H A S
V O C L A N A I E V T O S W E E P G G T
W J I S S F I L R S T N D Z G T Z I U A
C Q W F N I F N J E L A E R R O R E E R
C D V F O M S O N S S L A C A D Q X Q S
Z U P O I M G B L I D D Y I C C C Q X K
D Q U Y P M J O G L A N L N U C D F N L
G P A A M D V F A G A R E R N U B L U A
D Z M L A N C Y G T Q H T G O Y B G I B
R D L P H F B P I D S C J X E W R P N W
C L U T C H C R E S O L C Y E L N N U S
```

Try to find all the words contained in the list below: (Hint: Words may be found by looking up and down, across, or diagonally. Some words are even spelled backwards!)

WORLDSERIES	SWEEP	AMERICAN	LEAGUE	ERROR
WILDCARD	CLOSER	NATIONAL	LEGENDS	CURSES
PLAYOFFS	EXTRAINNINGS	ALLSTARS	GOATS	CHAMPIONS
CLUTCH	DIVISION	HALLOFFAMER	VILLAINS	EIGHTYSIX

Solution is on page 57.

You Make the Call #2

Ball or strike? Fair or Foul? Safe or Out? Usually, the umpires have to make the tough decisions, but now... YOU MAKE THE CALL!

Here's the situation...

There's one out in the bottom of the seventh inning at Yankee Stadium. Melky Cabrera is at first base and Jorge Posada is awaiting the pitch in the batter's box. Joe Girardi, from the bench, sends in a sign for a "hit and run" to the third base coach, who then relays Girardi's play to the runner (Cabrera) and the hitter (Posada). As the pitcher winds up, Melky takes off for second; Posada, knowing he must swing or Cabrera will be thrown out, takes a hack at a pitch outside the strike zone.

On this day in the Bronx, however, the wind is blowing out to right: Posada's desperation swing hits the ball directly into the wind and is pushed just over the right field fence for a home run! Melky, who was sprinting to second, took his eyes off the base he was running towards to watch the ball barely clear the wall. Melky jumped in the air in celebration, but did not notice how close he was to the bag. When he lands, his cleat gets caught on second base, twisting his ankle so he cannot move. Posada—taking care not to pass Melky on the bases—can only watch as the runner in front of him lies on the ground.

Is it a home run if the runner on base cannot score? Must Posada—even though he hit one over the fence—stay at first with a single so he doesn't pass the runner in front of him?

Solution is on page 57.

Retired Numbers at *Yankee Stadium* Matching Game

Match the famous the player or manager below with the retired number that they wore on the ball field. Enter the name of the player below the uniform containing their number on the next page.

Ron Guidry-P
Won the 1978 Cy Young with a 25-3 record

Casey Stengel-Manager
The only manager to win five straight World Series, 1949-53

Yogi Berra-C
Beginning in 1946, spent nineteen years as a Yankees catcher, winning ten World Series

Babe Ruth-OF
Hit 714 home runs, a one-time record

Thurman Munson-C
Was the catcher on the 1976-78 teams, during which the Yankees won three pennants and two World Series championships

Joe Dimaggio-OF
Hit in 56 straight games

Lou Gehrig- 1B
Played in 2,130 straight games, a one-time record

Phil Rizzuto-SS
Earned the 1951 World Series MVP and spent 40 years as a Yankees broadcaster after retirement

Jackie Robinson-2b
Was the first African-American in Major League Baseball history

Whitey Ford-P
Threw 33 consecutive scoreless innings in World Series games

Bill Dickey-C
Caught more than 100 games in thirteen straight seasons, 1929-42

Billy Martin-Manager/IF
Won four World Series rings as a player and won one as manager

Elston Howard-C
First African-American player in Yankees history

Reggie Jackson-OF
Nicknamed "Mr. October" for blasting three homers for the Yankees in game 6 of the 1977 World Series

Roger Maris-OF
Broke Babe Ruth's record by hitting 61 homers in 1961

Mickey Mantle-OF
Won Three American League MVP's and played in 16 MLB All-Star Game exhibitions

Don Mattingly-1B
1985 American League MVP who won nine Gold Gloves

Retired Numbers at *Yankee Stadium* Matching Game

Solution is on page 58.

Use your knowledge about baseball terminology to solve the following crossword puzzle.

Crossword Puzzle 4 - Baseball Terminology

Across

1. The _____ hitter takes the place of the pitcher in A.L. lineups.
3. The Brewers, Pirates, and Cubs play in the N.L. _____ Division.
4. Lefty pitchers usually are better at _____ off runners than righties.
6. When it's going to be a close play, _____ into a base might get you there quicker.
8. Whenever a multicolored _____ falls from the stands onto the field, the game has to pause until the ball boy pops it.
10. The third base coach will use his arms to ____ a runner home.
13. Foul balls, programs, ticket stubs, and pennants are all great _____ to take home from the ballpark.
15. From first base to second base, it is _____ feet.
17. When a pitcher throws this pitch he won't use his fingertips and wants as little spin on the ball as possible.
18. Teams that have stadiums with _____ roofs can enjoy the sun and still play when it rains.
19. "It was almost a home run, but it landed on the dirt _____." (Two Words)

Down

2. Baseball players often chew _____ seeds in the dugout.
5. The catcher's ribs are protected by his _____. (Two Words)
7. Before the World Series and League Championship Series, the eight playoff teams play in the _____ Series.
9. If they have time, most Major Leaguers are happy to ____ balls and baseball cards for their fans.
11. When the manager gets ejected, usually the _____ coach steps in for him.
12. If a player gets a lot of walks and hits, he has a great On Base _____.
14. The foul lines are made of this.
16. Some players rub _____ on their bats for a better grip.

- 34 -

Crossword Puzzle 4 - Baseball Terminology

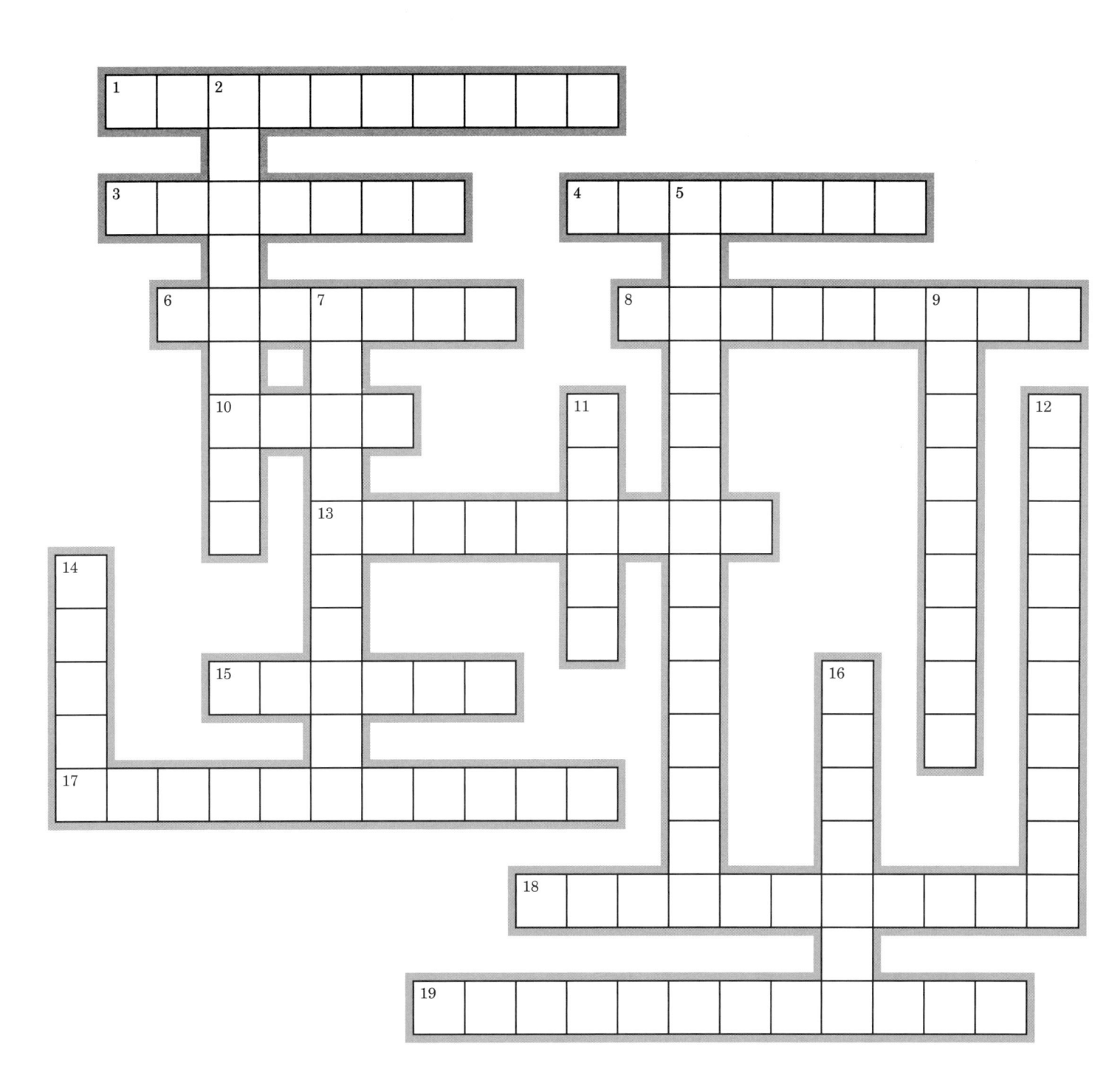

Solution is on page 58.

Jorge Posada watches his hit soar into the sky, hoping it clears the wall for another clutch home run.

A-Rod glides to his left to gobble up another grounder for an easy out.

Word Search #3
World Series MVPs

```
G L Q V H L O I X B Y Q R X S H V Z U M
D G L H I R L I K T X E T T E K C E B P
L G T Y J O X E H L S E Y C R L M I K E
T N S E D P L G M I N E G A H R E B A S
C I Z S O Y I A H M H M E N I V A L G C
K L U P T N R S Z Y A G O W V X C W P N
T L T M K N R H F E L R F R T W J Z R H
T I S E R E T E J A R K T R R T L I H I
T H R D H J O V U Z D I A E O I S J U H
W C E N J O R S S K V W M L Y T S O L N
P S D T S H J M W Q E E W A T D I J W D
O C R B B N C Z K T L C Q S R S V L H N
R I O G H S U Z S X M A R I V E R A O D
T F B W G O N F O N I E T S K C E G L M
E Q Z E D N A N R E H U J Z Y L A J W P
R C X D W E T T E L A N D S U I S O R B
```

Try to find all the words contained in the list below: (Hint: Words may be found by looking up and down, across, or diagonally. Some words are even spelled backwards!)

ECKSTEIN	SCHILLING	HERNANDEZ	MORRIS	KNIGHT
DYE	JOHNSON	WETTELAND	RIJO	SABERHAGEN
RAMIREZ	JETER	GLAVINE	STEWART	TRAMMELL
BECKETT	RIVERA	MOLITOR	HERSHISER	DEMPSEY
GLAUS	BROSIUS	BORDERS	VIOLA	PORTER

Solution is on page 59.

Maze

Master the maze to help Bobby Abreu send the ball to the fan in the upper deck!

Solution is on page 59.

- 39 -

Connect-the-Dots #2

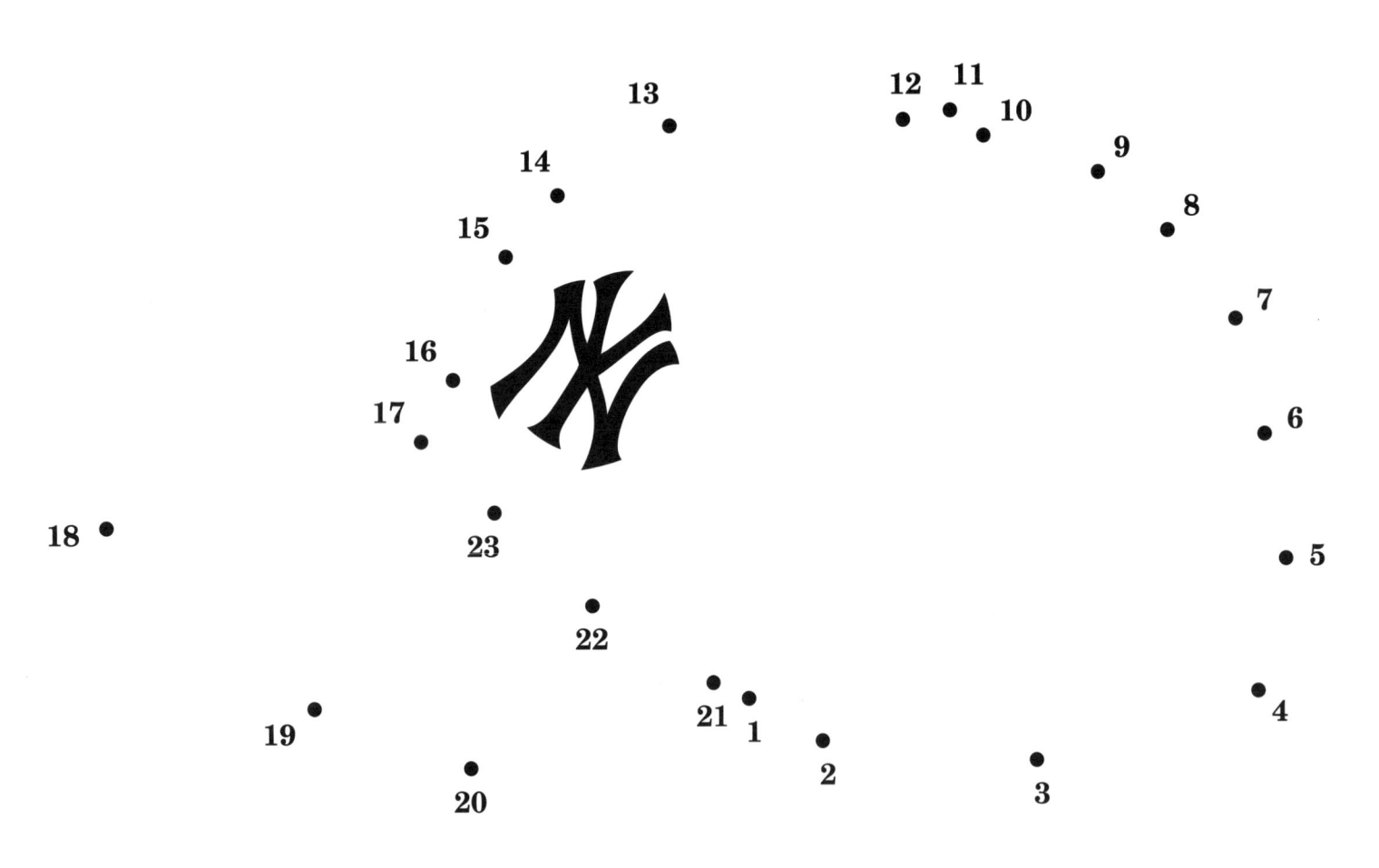

Worn by young and old, this is the sign of a true *Yankees* fan.

- 40 -

Jason Giambi's powerful swing sends another pitch into the Yankee Stadium upper deck.

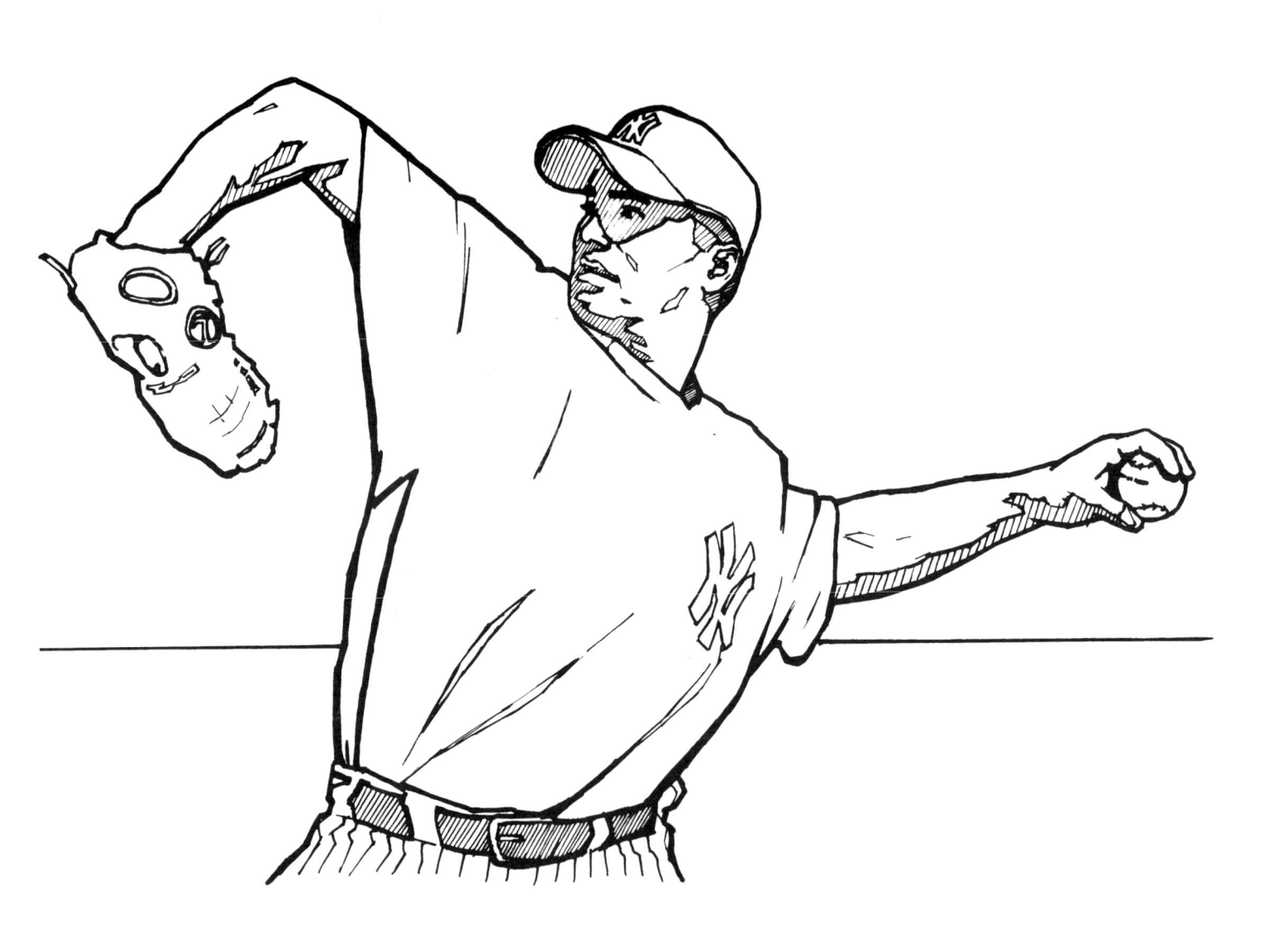

Big game heroics come natural to lefty Andy Pettitte.

Hideki Matsui unleashes a monstrous swing that sends a pitch deep into the stands.

Bobby Abreu's eyes concentrate on the bat meeting the ball for another line drive.

Yankees pitcher Phil Hughes is a phenom waiting to show the world what he can do.

Use your knowledge about *Major League Baseball* teams to solve the following crossword puzzle.

Crossword Puzzle 5 - *Major League Baseball* Teams

Across

1 This team used to hail from Brooklyn, NY.

4 This team played in Philadelphia and Kansas City before moving to the West Coast.

7 This team used to play in Montreal, Canada.

8 This team has won two World Series titles, even though they've only existed since 1993.

9 This team had Roberto Clemente in its outfield for 18 years.

12 This team from the "Land of a Thousand Lakes" plays in the Hubert H. Humphrey Metrodome.

13 This team is located right next to Disneyland.

14 This team has won a record 26 World Series titles.

15 This N.L. East Division team calls Shea Stadium home.

19 This team hails from the North Side of the Windy City.

21 This A.L. East team used to be called the St. Louis Browns.

23 This is the only team that presently plays its home games outside the United States.

24 This National League team retired the number "19" in honor of Tony Gwynn.

25 This N.L. Central team was referred to as "Big Red Machine" in the 1970's.

26 This team from the N.L. West Division is named after a mountain range.

27 In the A.L. West Division, this team won 116 games in 2001, tying a regular season record.

28 It took them 86 years, but this team finally won another World Series title in 2004.

Down

1 This A.L. East Division team joined the league in 1998.

2 You might recognize this team from their "Phanatic" mascot.

3 Barry Bonds broke the single-season and all time home run record while playing left field for this team.

5 With 10 victories, this team has won the most World Series titles in the National League, most recently in 2006.

6 This team's original name was the "Colt .45's."

10 This team used to be the Washington Senators before moving to the "Lone Star State."

11 This team won the World Series in 2001, despite having only come into the league in 1998.

16 After losing over 100 games in 2002 and 2003, this team reached the World Series in 2006.

17 Look for this team on the South side of the Windy City.

18 Before the 1998 season, this team switched from the American League Central to the National League Central.

20 This team won the National League East Division 13 straight years before failing to do so in 2006.

22 This team had to play a "home" series of games in Milwaukee because of extreme snowfall during the '07 season.

Use your knowledge about *Major League Baseball* teams to solve the following crossword puzzle.

Crossword Puzzle 5 - *Major League Baseball* Teams

Solution is on page 60.

- 47 -

Jorge Posada springs out of his catcher's crouch to nail an attempted base stealer.

You Make the Call #3

Ball or strike? Fair or Foul? Safe or Out? Usually, the umpires have to make the tough decisions, but now... YOU MAKE THE CALL!

Here's the situation...

Yankees starter Andy Pettitte was pitching in Yankee Stadium on a rainy day in April. After four innings of shutout ball against the Orioles, Pettitte was removed from the game in the fifth after walking the bases loaded. Luckily Brian Bruney came in to finish out the inning without allowing a run. The Yankees led 2-0 when a downpour occurred after the top of the sixth. The umpire had no choice but to call the game. Since the game had progressed past 5 and 1/2 innings, it was an official Yankees win. However, who gets the win for the Yankees? Does Pettitte get the win even though a starter is supposed to complete five innings to earn one? Does Bruney get the win for pitching the last two innings, even though Pettitte came out with a lead that was never lost? Does the game being shortened by rain affect the decision?

Solution is on page 60.

Robinson Cano ignores the runner barreling towards him to turn the tough double play.

Test your *Yankees* knowledge by entering the name of the player who holds the *Yankees* records listed below:

- Most Hits in a Season: _____
- Most Stolen Bases in a Season: _____
- Most RBI with the Yankees: _____
- Most Home Runs in a Season: _____
- Most At Bats with the Yankees: _____
- Lowest ERA in a Season: _____
- Most Wins with the Yankees: _____
- Most Saves in a Season: _____
- Most Strikeouts with the Yankees: _____
- Most Strikeouts in a Season: _____

Solution is on page 60.

Two Yankees leaders, Jeter (right) and Rodriguez, remain focused on the game at all times.

Solutions to Puzzles
Crossword Puzzle 1, page 5 - *Yankee Stadium* Facts

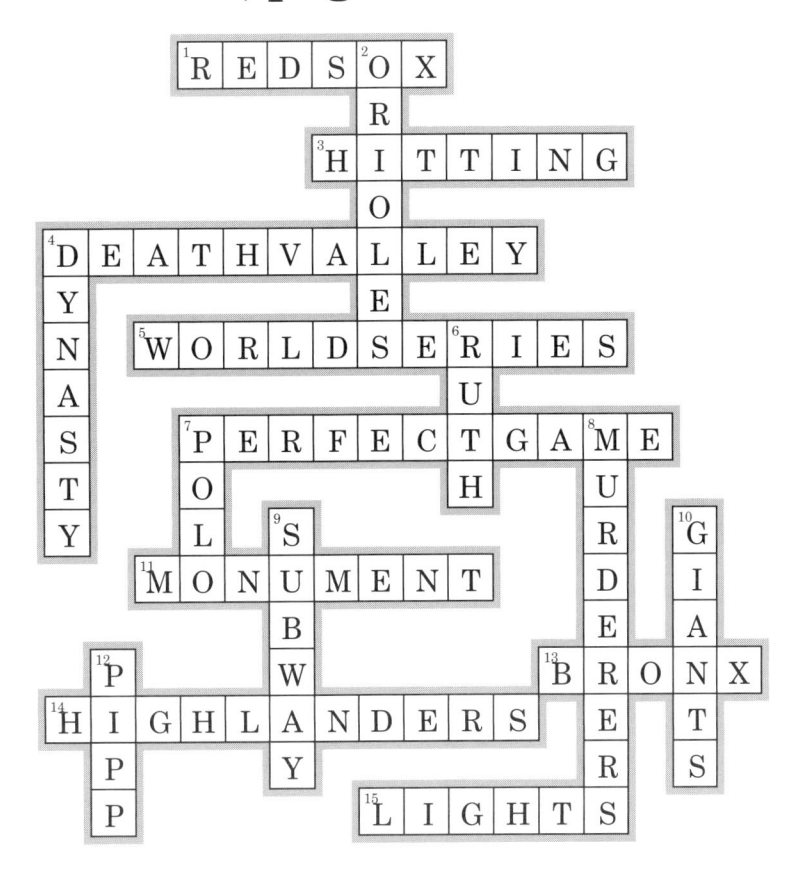

Across / Down answers (filled grid):

- 1. REDSOX
- 2. ORIOLE
- 3. HITTING
- 4. DEATHVALLEY / DYNASTY
- 5. WORLDSERIES
- 6. RUTH
- 7. PERFECTGAME / POL
- 8. MURDERER
- 9. SUBWAY
- 10. GIANTS
- 11. MONUMENT
- 12. PIPP
- 13. BRONX / BERER
- 14. HIGHLANDERS
- 15. LIGHTS

Solution to Word Search #1, page 9:
The Greatest *Yankees* Players

Try to find all the words contained in the list below: (Hint: Words may be found by looking up and down, across, or diagonally. Some words are even spelled backwards!)

RUTH	MANTLE	FORD	HOWARD	PETTITTE
DIMAGGIO	BERRA	MATTINGLY	DICKEY	WINFIELD
GEHRIG	RIZZUTO	JACKSON	ONEILL	GOMEZ
MARIS	MUNSON	MARTIN	GUIDRY	HUNTER

- 53 -

Solution to *Yankees* Player Challenge, page 11

1. Alex Rodriguez
2. Jorge Posada
3. Derek Jeter
4. Bobby Abreu
5. Robinson Cano
6. Johnny Damon
7. Hideki Matsui
8. Melky Cabrera
9. Mike Mussina
10. Chien-Ming Wang
11. Andy Pettitte
12. Mariano Rivera

Solution to Crossword Puzzle 2, page 13
Yankees Players

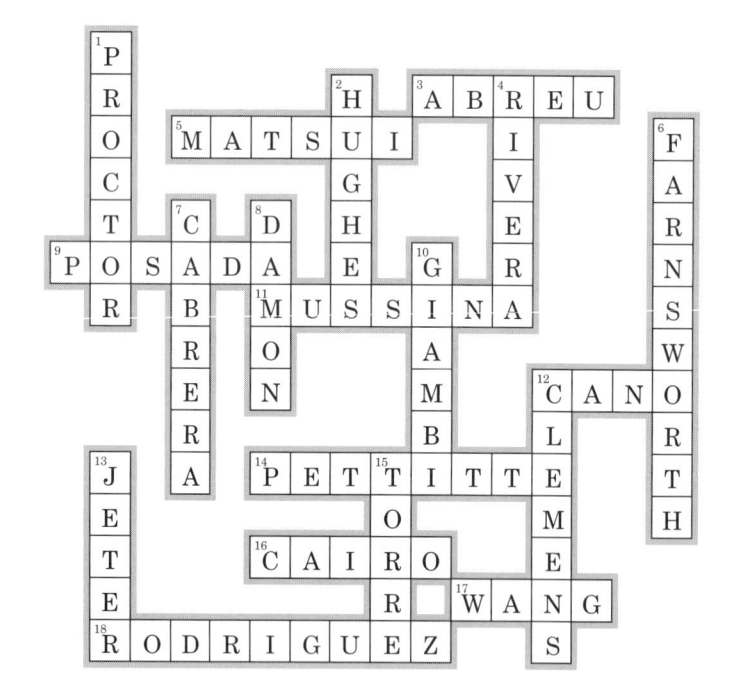

			¹P													
			R				²H		³A	⁴B	R	E	U			
			O		⁵M	A	T	S	U	I					⁶F	
			C				G			V					A	
			T		⁷C		⁸D	H		E					R	
		⁹P	O	S	A	D	A			¹⁰G					N	
			R		B		¹¹M	U	S	S	I	N	A		S	
					R		O			A					W	
					E		N			M		¹²C	A	N	O	
					R					B		L			R	
		¹³J		A		¹⁴P	E	T	¹⁵T	I	T	T	E		T	
		E						O			M			H	
		T		¹⁶C	A	I	R	O		E				
		E				R		¹⁷W	A	N	G			
		¹⁸R	O	D	R	I	G	U	E	Z		S			

Solution to You Make the Call #1, page 17

The Umpire will say: "Game over. **Yankees** win!" It doesn't matter if a pitch hits you—if you swing, you're out. LaRoche was fooled by the cutter and swung. What happens after that doesn't matter. Rivera picks up the strikeout and the Yankees walk away with a hard-fought win.

Solution to solve the *Yankees* Scramble, page 18

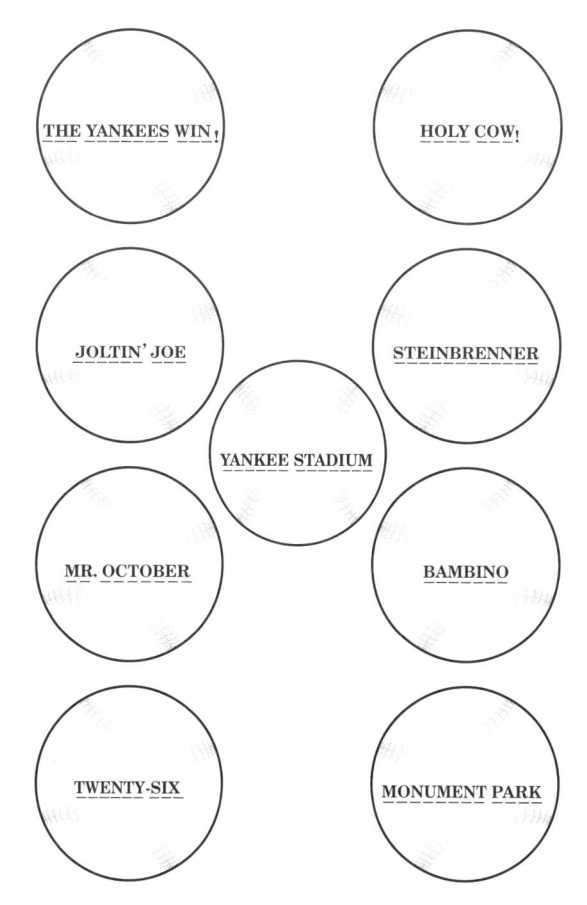

- THE YANKEES WIN!
- HOLY COW!
- JOLTIN' JOE
- STEINBRENNER
- YANKEE STADIUM
- MR. OCTOBER
- BAMBINO
- TWENTY-SIX
- MONUMENT PARK

Solution to solve the *Yankees* Nicknames, page 21

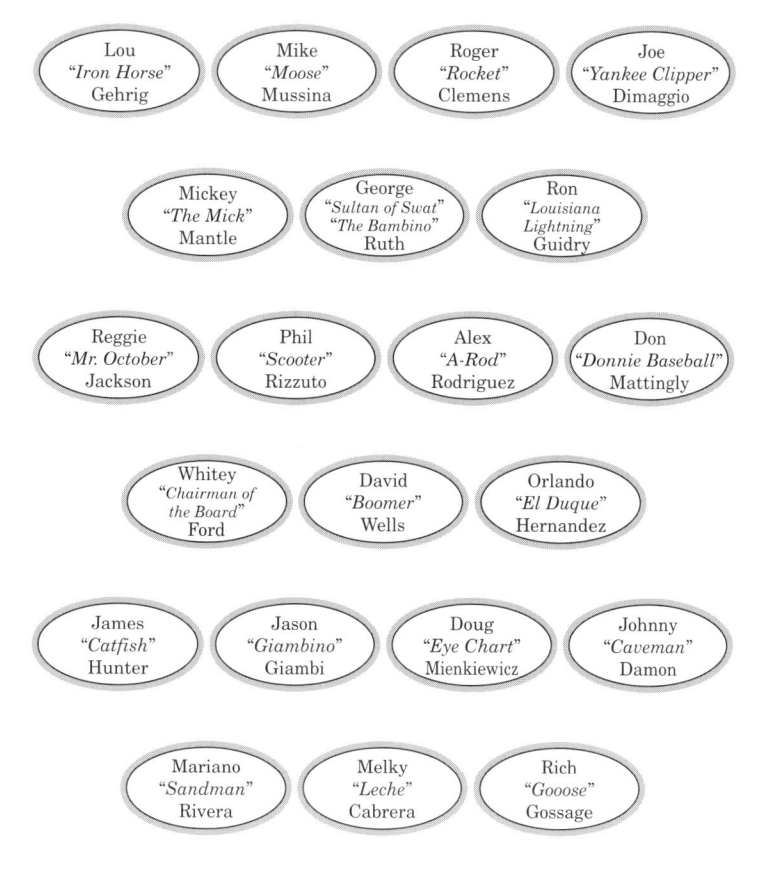

- Lou "Iron Horse" Gehrig
- Mike "Moose" Mussina
- Roger "Rocket" Clemens
- Joe "Yankee Clipper" Dimaggio
- Mickey "The Mick" Mantle
- George "Sultan of Swat" "The Bambino" Ruth
- Ron "Louisiana Lightning" Guidry
- Reggie "Mr. October" Jackson
- Phil "Scooter" Rizzuto
- Alex "A-Rod" Rodriguez
- Don "Donnie Baseball" Mattingly
- Whitey "Chairman of the Board" Ford
- David "Boomer" Wells
- Orlando "El Duque" Hernandez
- James "Catfish" Hunter
- Jason "Giambino" Giambi
- Doug "Eye Chart" Mienkiewicz
- Johnny "Caveman" Damon
- Mariano "Sandman" Rivera
- Melky "Leche" Cabrera
- Rich "Gooose" Gossage

Solution to Crossword Puzzle 3, page 23
Yankees Dynasty

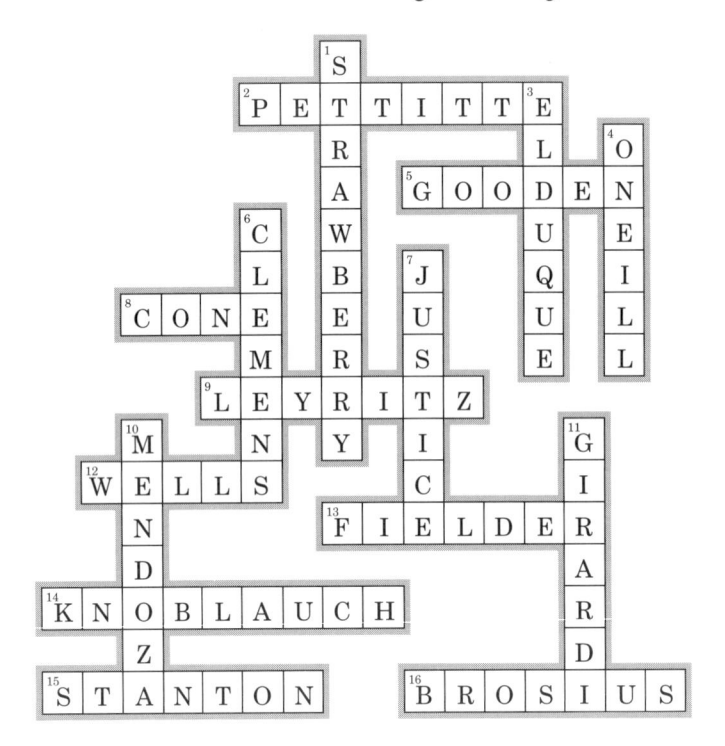

Across: 2. PETTITTE, 5. GOODEN, 8. CONE, 9. LEYRITZ, 12. WELLS, 13. FIELDER, 14. KNOBLAUCH, 15. STANTON, 16. BROSIUS

Down: 1. STRAWBERRY, 3. ELUQUE, 4. ONEILL, 6. CLEMENS, 7. JUSTICE, 10. MENDOZA, 11. GIRARDI

Solution to International Game, page 27

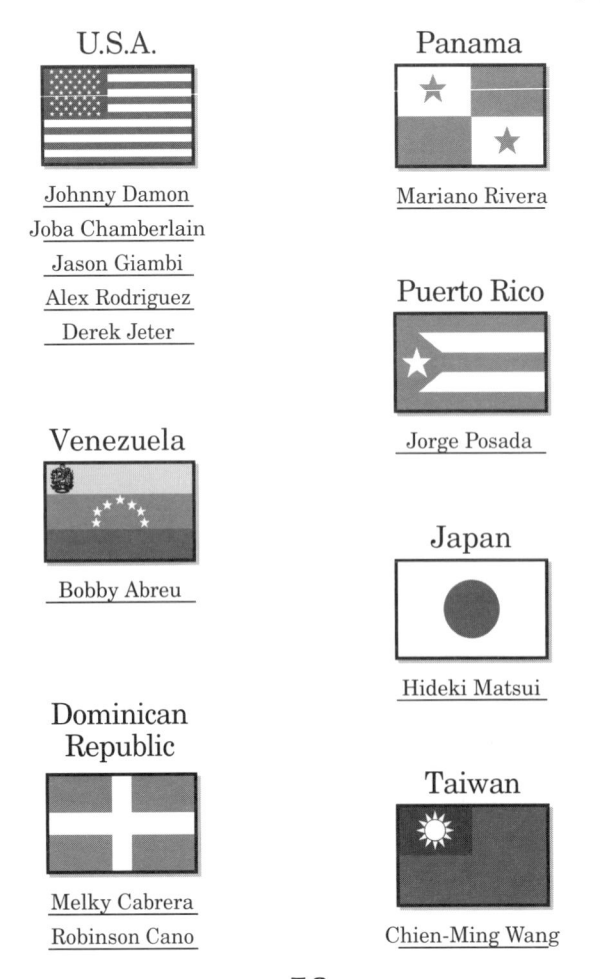

U.S.A.
Johnny Damon
Joba Chamberlain
Jason Giambi
Alex Rodriguez
Derek Jeter

Panama
Mariano Rivera

Puerto Rico
Jorge Posada

Venezuela
Bobby Abreu

Japan
Hideki Matsui

Dominican Republic
Melky Cabrera
Robinson Cano

Taiwan
Chien-Ming Wang

Solution to Word Search #2 - October Baseball, page 30

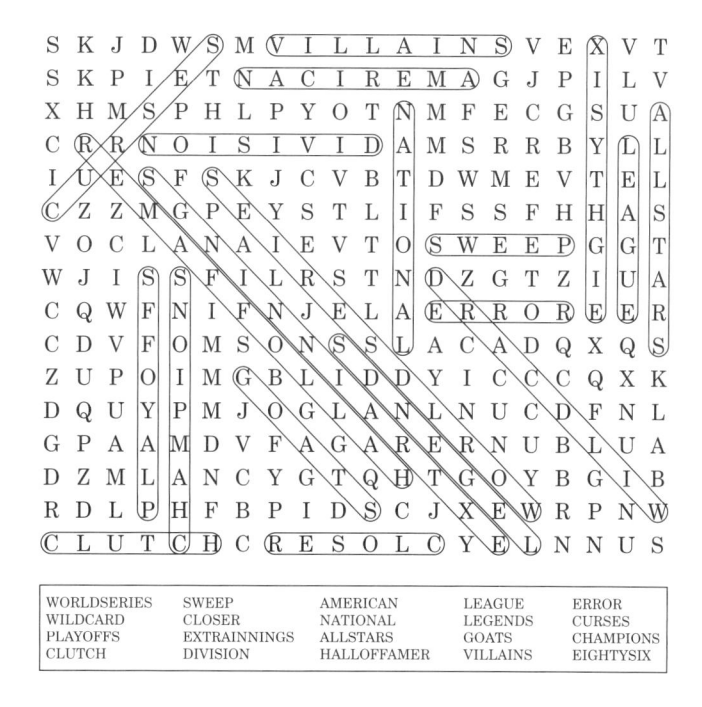

```
S K J D W S M V I L L A I N S V E X V T
S K P I E T N A C I R E M A G J P I L V
X H M S P H L P Y O T N M F E C G S U A
C R R N O I S I V I D A M S R R B Y T L
I U E S F S K J C V B T D W M E V T E L
C Z Z M G P E Y S T L I F S S F H A G S
V O C L A N A I E V T O S W E E P G G T
W J I S F I L R S T N D Z G T Z I U U A
C Q W F N I F N J E L A E R R O R E E R
C D V F O M S O N S S L A C A D Q X Q S
Z U P O I M G B L I D D Y I C C Q X K
D Q U Y P M J O G L A N L N U C D F N L
G P A A M D V F A G A R E R N U B L U A
D Z M L A N C Y G T Q H T G O Y B G I B
R D L P H F B P I D S C J X E W R P N W
C L U T C H C R E S O L C Y E L N N U S
```

WORLDSERIES	SWEEP	AMERICAN	LEAGUE	ERROR
WILDCARD	CLOSER	NATIONAL	LEGENDS	CURSES
PLAYOFFS	EXTRAINNINGS	ALLSTARS	GOATS	CHAMPIONS
CLUTCH	DIVISION	HALLOFFAMER	VILLAINS	EIGHTYSIX

Solution to You Make the Call #2, page 31

The Yankees would be allowed to enter a pinch runner for the injured Cabrera. Even though the new runner is technically being entered in the middle of the play, it is allowed. Posada would watch as the new runner enters the game, and then follow him around the bases. Posada is credited with a home run, two RBI, and a run scored. The new runner is credited with scoring a run.

- 57 -

Solution to Retired Numbers, page 33

1	Billy Martin
3	Babe Ruth
4	Lou Gehrig
5	Joe Dimaggio
7	Mickey Mantle
8	Bill Dickey
8	Yogi Berra
9	Roger Maris
10	Phill Rizzuto
15	Thurman Munson
16	Whitey Ford
23	Don Mattingly
32	Elston Howard
37	Casey Stengel
42	Jackie Robinson
44	Reggie Jackson
49	Ron Guidry

Solution to Crossword Puzzle 4, page 35
Baseball Terminology

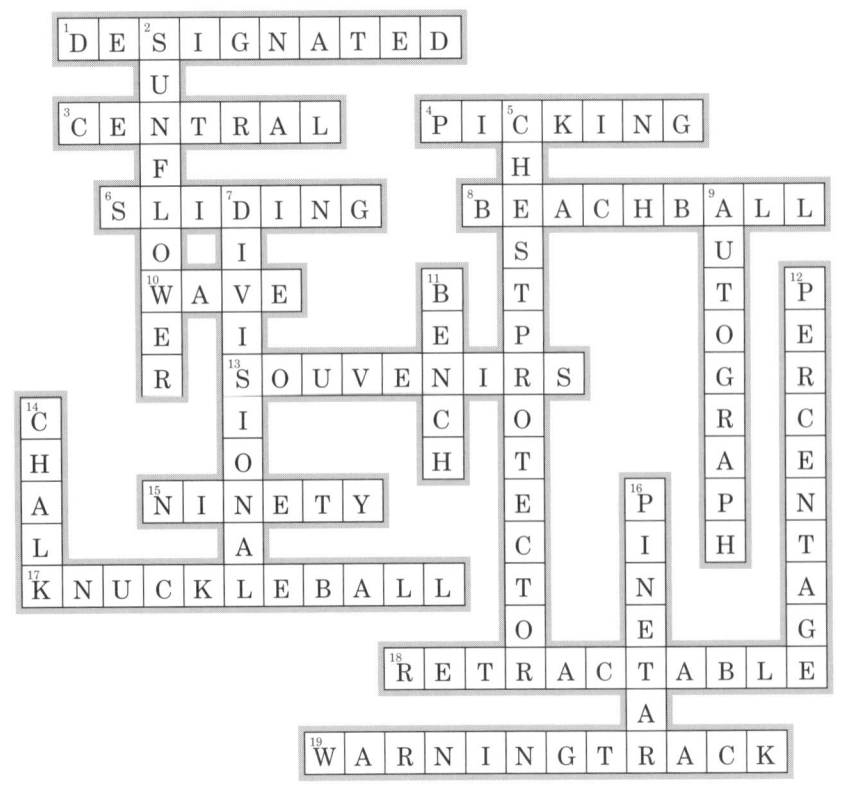

Across / Down answers:
- DESIGNATED
- CENTRAL
- PICKING
- SLIDING
- BEACHBALL
- WAVE
- SOUVENIRS
- NINETY
- KNUCKLEBALL
- RETRACTABLE
- WARNINGTRACK
- DUFFOS (DUFF...)
- CHUFF
- PITCH
- BENCH
- PROTECTOR
- AUTOGRAPH
- PERCENTAGE
- CHALK
- PINE
- RETRACTA
- SION
- BESTPOT...

- 58 -

Solution to Word Search #3, page 38 - *World Series* MVPs

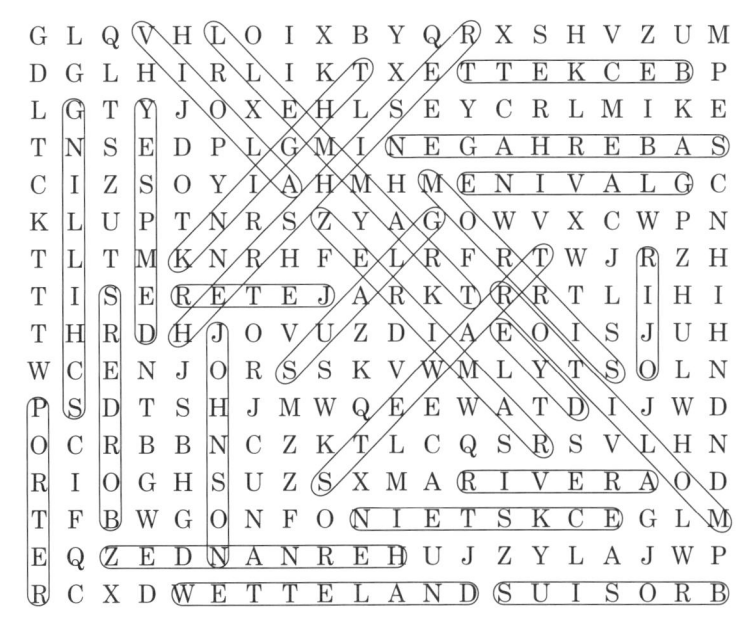

Try to find all the words contained in the list below: (Hint: Words may be found by looking up and down, across, or diagonally. Some words are even spelled backwards!)

ECKSTEIN	SCHILLING	HERNANDEZ	MORRIS	KNIGHT
DYE	JOHNSON	WETTELAND	RIJO	SABERHAGEN
RAMIREZ	JETER	GLAVINE	STEWART	TRAMMELL
BECKETT	RIVERA	MOLITOR	HERSHISER	DEMPSEY
GLAUS	BROSIUS	BORDERS	VIOLA	PORTER

Solution to Maze, page 39

- 59 -

Solution to Crossword Puzzle 5, page 47
Major League Baseball Teams

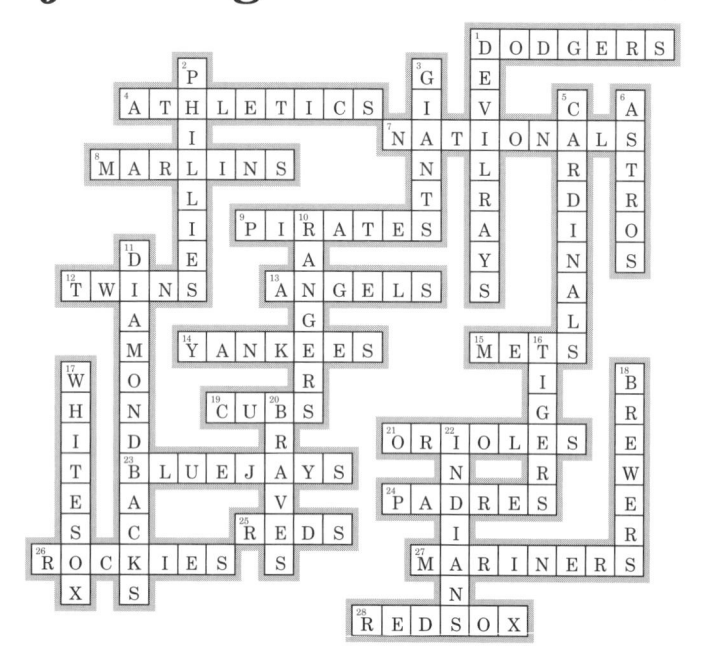

Solution to solve the *Yankees* records, page 51

Most Hits in a Season	238	Don Mattingly (1986)
Most Stolen Bases in a Season	93	Rickey Henderson (1988)
Most RBI with the Yankees	1,995	Lou Gehrig
Most Home Runs in a Season	659	Babe Ruth
Most At Bats with the Yankees	8102	Mickey Mantle
Lowest ERA in a Season	2.14	Rich Gossage
Most Wins with the Yankees	41	Jack Chesbro (1904)
Most Saves in a Season	53	Mariano Rivera (2004)
Most Strikeouts with the Yankees	1,956	Whitey Ford
Most Strikeouts in a Season	9	Ron Guidry (1978)

Solution to You Make the Call #3, page 49

Pettitte does get the win. Rain-shortened 5 inning games only require the starter to throw 4, not 5, innings to earn a win. Bruney would have earned the win had the score stayed the same throughout a normal nine-inning game.

We hope that you enjoyed the second edition of the
New York Yankees Coloring and Activity Book!

Please contact us with questions or comments at:

Hawk's Nest Publishing LLC
84 Library Street
Mystic, CT 06355
www.HawksNestPublishing.com

Hawk's Nest Publishing, LLC

Books for the Young and Young at Heart...

To order additional copies of this book:

Phone Pathway Book Service
800-345-6665 or 603-357-0236

Web www.HawksNestPublishing.com

Mail Hawk's Nest Publishing
c/o Pathway Book Service
P.O. Box 89
Gilsum, NH 03448

Hawk's Nest Publishing, LLC

Books for the Young and Young at Heart...

HawksNestPublishing.com